Power Hat Panic

Kate Saunders worked as an actress until she was twenty-five and then became a writer. She has written five novels and edited a collection of short stories. As a journalist she has worked for the *Sunday Times*, the *Daily Telegraph*, the *Independent* and the *Sunday Express*, and is currently writing a weekly column in the *Express*. She can be heard regularly on BBC Radio 4, presenting *Woman's Hour* and appearing on *Start the Week* and *Front Row*. She lives in London and has a six-year-old son.

The *Belfry Witches* titles are Kate's first books for children. A major BBC TV series is based on them.

D1434588

Titles in The Belfry Witches series

All Belfry Witches titles can be ordered at
your local bookshop or are available by post
from Book Service by Post (tel: 01624 675137).

The Belfry Witches

Power Hat Panic

Kate Saunders
Illustrated by Tony Ross

MACMILLAN
CHILDREN'S BOOKS

20084129

For my nephews Tom and George

First published 2000 by Macmillan Children's Books
a division of Macmillan Publishers Limited
25 Eccleston Place, London SW1W 9NF
Basingstoke and Oxford
www.macmillan.co.uk

Associated companies throughout the world

ISBN 0 330 37285 8

3 5 7 9 8 6 4 2

A CIP catalogue record for this book is available from
the British Library.

Typeset by SX Composing DTP, Rayleigh, Essex
Printed and bound in Great Britain by Mackays of Chatham plc, Kent

Contents

1

The Old Bag is Dead

It was a bright autumn morning in the quiet village of Tranters End, but Skirty Marm could not enjoy it. She was in one of her Moods.

"It's NOT FAIR!" she thundered. "What's the point of choosing two witches to be god-mothers, if you won't let them give the baby a magic present?"

Old Noshie was sitting on her cushion, comfortably eating a bowl of flaked bats for her breakfast. "We promised Mr B.," she reminded her friend. "No more magic without written permission, unless it's an emergency."

"POOH!" shouted Skirty Marm. She began to pace up and down across the dusty floor of the church belfry where the two witches lived. "Everyone else will give Thomas boring rattles and shawls. I wanted to give that baby some-thing really special!"

The baby in question was Thomas William Babbercorn. He belonged to Mr Cuthbert Babbercorn, the young curate at St Tranter's Church, and his wife, Alice. Ever since Old Noshie and Skirty Marm had been thrown off Witch Island, Mr Babbercorn had been their best human friend. They loved Alice very nearly as much – they had been her bridesmaids, and a copy of the wedding photograph was taped to one of the huge church bells that hung above the witches' heads. Until the thrilling arrival of Thomas, it had been the happiest day of the witches' lives.

"I thought of another perfect gift last night," Skirty Marm said. "What if we gave Thomas the power to make himself INVISIBLE?"

Old Noshie was impressed. She always admired Skirty's ideas (sometimes with unfortunate consequences).

"Thomas would like that," she said slowly, thinking it over. "Especially when he gets bigger. If he didn't want to go to school one morning, he could just vanish!" She sighed, then shook her head. "But I don't think Alice would like having a vanishing baby. I think we should give Thomas the power to make himself FLY."

"You old fool!" snapped Skirty Marm. "She certainly doesn't want a flying baby. What if he fell asleep while he was on the ceiling? Alice and Mr B. would keep having to fetch the ladder!"

"Drat, I didn't think of that," Old Noshie said humbly.

"That's just your trouble," Skirty Marm said, in a stern voice. "You don't THINK, Noshie."

"I never was much good at it," admitted Old Noshie.

She was a plump easy-going witch, with startling, bright green skin. Her wrinkled head was completely bald, and she wore a blue wig under her pointed hat, to keep it warm. At Witch School she had trundled along at the bottom of the class, quite content to be in the shadow of her brilliant friend and cave-mate, Skirty Marm.

Skirty Marm was long and skinny. Her skin was grey, her eyes were red, and her hair was purple. When she was angry, or thinking very hard, sparks shot out of the ends of her hair. At school, she had won all kinds of dazzling prizes, including the Spellbinder's Medal for thirty-six years in a row. She never could accept Mr Babbercorn's strict "No Magic" rule.

"Cheer up, Skirt!" urged Old Noshie. "We'll be able to buy Thomas something lovely with all the human money we've saved. Our money-box is filling up nicely." She rattled the box, which was shaped like a little thatched cottage.

Mr Babbercorn had given them permission to use very mild magic, so that they could earn some human money by doing odd jobs for the people of the village. Mostly, this meant flying up to roofs on their broomsticks, and clearing blocked gutters or fixing television aerials. It was all rather a come-down for an award-winning Spellbinder like Skirty Marm.

She opened her mouth to insult Old Noshie. At that moment, however, something black and smoky suddenly crashed through the open belfry window.

Both witches coughed and spluttered as a cloud of smoke covered everything in a fine layer of black soot. When the smoke cleared, they saw a battered newspaper lying in the middle of the floor.

"Well I never!" cried Skirty Marm, forgetting to be cross. "It's the *Witch Island Courier*!"

This was the national newspaper of Witch

Island, the bleak and rocky land where the two witches had once lived.

Old Noshie squeaked and hid behind her friend – she was rather a coward. "What does it mean, Skirt? Who sent it?"

Skirty Marm was very brave. "It's been sent by Super-Express, and you know how much that costs," she said. "This must be something important."

She picked up the newspaper – still warm from its magical expressing – and opened it out.

"Aaargh!" yelled Old Noshie, her blue wig bristling with shock.

Plastered across the front page was a photograph of a disgusting old witch, with metal teeth and a coarse grey beard.

"Mrs Abercrombie," Skirty Marm said bitterly. "Our worst enemy!" Then her grey skin turned a dirty white. "Noshie! Look at the headline! 'EX-QUEEN VANISHES IN TUNNEL DISASTER!'"

In a shaking voice, she read out the story.

"The Witch Island Police yesterday gave up the search for disgraced former queen Mrs Abercrombie, reported missing after the shock collapse of three disused underground tunnels.

'It's now pretty certain that Mrs A. was trapped in one of the tunnels,' said our respected leader, Chancellor Badsleeves. 'And all sensible witches will rejoice that the nasty old bag is dead.'

Mrs Abercrombie, who wasted all her money trying to win back power, had been teaching at Witch-School to make ends meet. The alarm was raised when she failed to turn up for her favourite lesson, Punishment Hour. She was known to keep an underground vault near the site of the disaster.

Chancellor Badsleeves described her dis-

appearance as 'the end of an era', and added that there would be a State Funeral, with fireworks and dancing afterwards."

There was a long long silence. This was an incredible piece of news. The wicked former queen of Witch Island, who had sworn to kill Old Noshie and Skirty Marm, was dead. The two witches were only jolted out of their gaping astonishment when the church bells struck eleven, making the whole tower shake. As soon as the racket died away, Skirty Marm cried "HURRAH!" and turned sixteen cartwheels.

Old Noshie, too fat for cartwheels, did eleven somersaults and stood on her head (I should explain that though they were over one hundred and fifty years old, this is an extremely young and sprightly age for a witch). Then she got out some mouldy sausage rolls she had been saving for a special celebration. Celebrations did not come more special than this one.

The late Mrs Abercrombie had hated Old Noshie and Skirty Marm. She had banished them from Witch Island for singing a rude song about her at the Hallowe'en Ball. That was bad enough. They had led the Revolution that ended her cruel reign, and that was terrible. But it was not the worst thing they had done to her.

They had stolen the Power Hat.

The Power Hat was a pointed hat, two metres tall, with an everlasting candle burning at its tip. A gale could blow and a flood of water pour down on it, but this candle never went out. The Hat was immensely magic, and anyone who wore it had incredible power. Skirty and Noshie had snatched the Power Hat from the unsavoury head of Mrs Abercrombie and hidden it in Tranters End. The ex-queen had tried to win it back, but had always failed.

These days, it was disguised as a black-and-white bobble hat, which made it far easier to hide. It lived quietly in Mr Babbercorn's underwear drawer, bothering nobody. Since its arrival among the humans it was a changed Hat. It had, to Mrs Abercrombie's disgust, turned Good.

"Badsleeves must have sent that paper," said Skirty Marm. The democratically elected Chancellor of Witch Island was an old friend of the two witches. "Good old Baddy! We must go back to Witch Island for the funeral – I bet that'll be the best party ever!"

Old Noshie was thoughtful. "We could go

back to LIVE there if we wanted," she mused. "Her magic can't reach us now she's been squashed like a big fat beetle."

Skirty Marm scornfully tossed her purple hair. "I don't mind visiting the Island, but I wouldn't live there again – not if they gave us a luxury cave, with hot and cold running slime. It's much nicer here."

"I'd be homesick for the humans," Old Noshie agreed. "We were so frightened of being banished, but it was actually the best thing that ever happened to us."

The witches had grown to love living in an English village. Because of their strange mixture of ages – very old for humans, very young for witches – they had joined both the Brownies and the Old Folks' Drop-In Club. They could not make up their minds which they liked best. Skirty Marm loved to look at the Old Folks' photograph albums, and hear their stories about human history. Old Noshie's Brownie badge for tying knots was the first prize she had ever won – she was so proud of it, she had sewn it to her vest.

"I miss my spellbook, though," Skirty Marm said. "And my red stockings. The new ones

Brown Owl made for us just aren't the same."

I should explain that on Witch Island, a witch's stockings are her pride and joy. You can tell the age and status of a witch by the colour of her stockings. A baby witch, under one hundred years old, wears yellow stockings and learns Elementary Magic at Witch School. At the age of one hundred, a witch becomes a Red-Stocking. She is given a broom, a share of a cave and the Red-Stocking spellbook. On her two hundredth birthday the stockings become green, and the spellbook is more advanced. Finally, at the age of three hundred, a witch becomes a Purple-Stocking and is licensed to cast the most powerful spells of all.

Mrs Abercrombie had been the oldest, cleverest and wickedest Purple on the Island. During the seven centuries of her reign, the Purples had kept talking cats as slaves and bullied the younger witches – especially the Red-Stockings, who had a reputation for being cheeky and disobedient. Nowadays, the country was led by the Red-Stocking Badsleeves, the cat-slaves were free, and the Greens and Purples had to behave. They would probably behave even better now that their old leader had been squashed by a collapsing tunnel.

"I've missed this cookery page," Old Noshie said, leafing through the *Witch Island Courier*. "Look – a delicious recipe for Ant Crumble. You soften the ants in diesel-oil, add a grated conker—"

"Stop thinking of your stomach," said Skirty Marm, snatching the paper. "Let's go and tell Mr B. the good news!"

Mr Babbercorn and his vicar, Mr Snelling, had met the late Mrs Abercrombie. It had not been a pleasant experience.

"Great idea," Old Noshie said. "Won't he be pleased to hear that he never needs to worry about Mrs A. ever again?"

The two joyous witches ran down the one hundred and eighty-six belfry steps to the vicarage next door. In the kitchen, they found the curate and his wife. Mr Babbercorn, a pale and somewhat weedy young man, was making a cup of tea. His wife Alice, a sweet-faced young woman with curly brown hair, was putting baby clothes into the washing machine. Baby Thomas was asleep in his carrycot.

"Morning, witches," said Alice.

"Have some tea," said Mr Babbercorn. He

poured them each a cup of warm water and added a spoonful of soil from the potted geranium on the windowsill – he knew the witches could not abide human tea.

Old Noshie and Skirty Marm were far too excited to drink anything. Both talking at the same time, they blurted out the amazing news.

Mr Babbercorn was so shocked, he had to sit down. "That terrible evil witch – dead!"

"I know it's wrong to feel happy," Alice said, "but it's such a relief!"

Mrs Abercrombie had once turned Alice into a snail, and Alice still had ghastly dreams about finding herself with a pair of tiny horns and a shell again.

There was a squawk from the carrycot.

"Hello, Thomas," said Old Noshie.

"He wants to talk to us," said Skirty Marm.

Mr Babbercorn and Alice smiled at each other. The witches claimed that there was a language called "Babyspeak", which enabled them to talk to Thomas. His parents (though they should have known better) found this very difficult to believe. Mothers and fathers – even when they have friends who are witches – think nobody understands their baby better than they do. And the noises the witches made at Thomas sounded ridiculous.

"It's a shame you don't know Babyspeak," said Old Noshie. "Would you like us to give you a few lessons?"

Alice picked up her baby. "No thanks."

Over her shoulder, the red and crumpled face of Thomas looked as if it was trying to smile at the witches.

He made a noise, which sounded like "ARRR!"

Skirty Marm replied: "Aaar-EE!"

If Alice and Mr Babbercorn had understood Babyspeak, they would have known that Thomas was saying: "Hello, witches – isn't it a lovely morning?"

And they would have heard Skirty Marm saying: "Hello, Thomas. I hope we didn't wake you."

"Not at all," said Thomas. "I just can't settle today – I've got wind."

"Poor thing," said Alice, "he can't settle today. He's got wind."

(Perhaps she did not need to learn Babyspeak after all.)

She put Thomas into his little bouncy chair.

"Drat, she's putting me in that chair!" complained Thomas.

"She's got to finish her tea," Old Noshie pointed out, in Babyspeak. "Do be reasonable. She can't hold you all the time."

"WHY NOT?" shouted Thomas.

Alice kissed his head, which was as bald as Old Noshie's.

"Come on, crosspatch! It's only for a minute."

"Oh, all right," said Thomas. "If you get me my plastic horses."

"Maybe he wants his horses," said Alice. She found his string of coloured horses and clipped them to the bouncy chair.

"She learns very quickly, bless her," Thomas told the witches.

Mr Babbercorn was thinking about Mrs Abercrombie. "It wouldn't be suitable to celebrate," he murmured. "After all, it is a tragedy. Maybe I should hold a service of thanksgiving?"

The back door opened and in walked Mendax.

"This shopping weighs a ton. I need a nice sit-down and a saucer of milk."

Mendax was a small black cat. He had once been a cat-slave on Witch Island, and Mrs Abercrombie had sent him to Tranters End as a spy. Old Noshie and Skirty Marm had now forgiven him for his shady past (though Skirty was still a little suspicious), and Mr Snelling had adopted him. Mendax was very bossy and ruled the soft-hearted vicar with a paw of iron, but the two were devoted to each other.

Mendax was an extremely useful cat. He cooked brilliantly, polished the furniture, and did light shopping. Mr Snelling had given him a little blue cart, which he could drag along the village street. Everyone in Tranters End was now quite used to meeting Mendax in Mrs Tucker's Post Office and General Shop. He was a great gossip and knew everything that went on in the village.

"The old woodman's cottage in the forest has been sold," he mewed, lifting a packet of nappies out of his cart. "Nobody has seen the lady who bought it, but Mrs Tucker says she's very rich and rather delicate."

Thomas squawked again. This meant: "I bet that's one of your LIES!"

In Latin, Mendax means "Liar" – and the name suited the little cat perfectly. He was absolutely addicted to telling tall stories. When people pointed this out, however, he was always offended.

"My dear Thomas," he purred in Babyspeak, "when you know me better, you will realize I am the SOUL of TRUTH."

"Never mind that broken-down old cottage!" cried Skirty Marm. "We've got a REAL piece of news." And she slammed down the *Witch Island Courier*.

When Mendax saw the headline, his fur stood on end. He began to tremble all over.

"Dead? Mrs Abercrombie? Oh, it's too wonderful! I hardly dare to believe it!"

"We should have a party," said Old Noshie. "With nice games and funny hats."

Mr Babbercorn was uneasy. "I really don't think that would be in the best of taste—" he began.

"Pooh to the best of taste!" said Mendax, recovering. He took his apron off its low hook beside the door. "I'll start the cake now! What do you fancy, witches – strawberry or chocolate?"

2

Mrs Brightpie

Mr Babbercorn felt rather guilty about being so happy, but nobody else did. Even the vicar, podgy Mr Snelling, who was one of the kindest men in the world, treated the fatal squashing of Mrs Abercrombie as a fine excuse for a party.

"I'm afraid I can't help it," he told Mr Babbercorn firmly. "Vicars aren't supposed to be pleased about things like this – but ever since that horrid old witch smashed her way into my house, I've been terrified that she'll come back. Now that she's gone, I'm just thankful to be safe."

"I never liked the idea that she might be using her spells to spy on us," admitted Mr Babbercorn. "The fact is, if people want anyone to be sorry at their funerals, they should be nicer when they're alive."

"Very true," said Mr Snelling. "I may get

Mendax to write me a sermon about it."

The sermons the vicar wrote himself were dull and waffly. The people of Tranters End had been delighted when Mendax started writing them instead. Mendax's sermons were sometimes rather far-fetched, but they were never boring.

"In the meantime," Mr Snelling went on, "let the witches have their celebration. Tell them they can play loud music on their transistor radio, and put fairy-lights on the bells."

Mendax cooked a splendid feast of cake, trifle and caramelized cockroaches, and danced with the witches far into the night.

This was the beginning of a very happy time at Tranters End. The October weather was as mild as spring. The autumn woods were every shade of red. Mr Babbercorn found himself singing as he delivered parish magazines. Mendax told fewer lies, the witches only quarrelled twice a day and Mr Snelling decided to hold a grand Harvest Supper.

"We need to raise some money for a new organ," he said, "and people always enjoy a feast. I'm hoping Mrs Brightpie will come."

Mrs Brightpie was the lady who had bought the ruined cottage in the middle of the woods.

She was a pretty old lady, with snow-white hair, pink cheeks and blue eyes. Though she looked delicate and walked with the help of a stick, she was very energetic and cheerful.

The cottage was right at the heart of the thick forest, but for several weeks lorries had been bringing in bricks and cement, and huge diggers had been squeezing down the narrow woodland paths. Mrs Brightpie was rich and she was turning the tumbledown old place into a dream home stuffed with luxuries.

Not that anyone in the village had seen it yet.

"I don't want to show it off until it's completely finished," Mrs Brightpie had laughed, while she was buying stamps from Mrs Tucker at the post office. "Then I'll hold a big housewarming party!"

Everyone looked forward to this. Mrs Brightpie had only been in Tranters End for a short time, but her kindness and generosity had made her very popular. She had bought a new papier-mâché toadstool for the Brownies to dance round, after the top fell off the old one. She had given the church a beautiful new tea urn, and she kept the Old Folks' Drop-In Club supplied with delicious biscuits (greedy old

Noshie, who loved human biscuits, was particularly pleased about this).

"What a super idea!" Mrs Brightpie exclaimed, when Mr Snelling told her about the Harvest Supper. "Of course I'll come – and I'll start off that organ fund with two hundred pounds!"

She would not let the vicar thank her.

"Nonsense, Mr Snelling. I have plenty to spare, and I believe in sharing. I want to do some good in this charming village."

Mrs Tucker said Mrs Brightpie was "a ray of sunshine".

Mr Snelling said, "How lucky we are, to have a kind-hearted neighbour like Mrs Brightpie!"

Mr Babbercorn and Alice liked her because she kissed Thomas and gave him a little velvet dinosaur.

Old Noshie and Skirty Marm liked her because she had not been at all shocked when the vicar explained about the two local witches and the talking cat.

"How fascinating!" she had cried, in her silvery voice. "I certainly don't mind a touch of magic. I shall enjoy chatting with Mendax. And Old Noshie and Skirty Marm must have tea with me, to tell me all about being witches!"

Since Mrs Brightpie's house was not ready yet, she held her special witches' tea at the vicarage. They were a little shy at first – Old Noshie, in particular, found human table manners very hard work, and they both wanted to make a good impression on the refined Mrs Brightpie.

But it was impossible to be shy for long. Mrs Brightpie was so interested and so sympathetic that they were soon treating her like an old friend. They even sang her "A Nasty Old Thing" – the rude song about Mrs Abercrombie that had got them banished from Witch Island.

"Goodness, how amusing!" laughed Mrs Brightpie. "I bet she was cross!"

"That's nothing!" boasted Old Noshie. "We stole her Power Hat!"

Mrs Brightpie handed her another chocolate biscuit. "Gosh, you must be very clever witches! What did you do with it?"

"We hid it in—" began Old Noshie.

Skirty Marm nudged her. "We'd better not tell you," she said quickly. "The Hat's a dangerous thing to know about."

Mrs Brightpie smiled. "Surely it doesn't matter, now that your queen is dead?"

"Some other witch might be after it," Skirty Marm said darkly. "And we'd hate to get you into trouble."

"You're very considerate," said Mrs Brightpie. For a moment she looked thoughtful. Then she smiled again and started talking about the Brownies. This was Old Noshie's favourite subject and she quickly forgot about the Power Hat.

"We always have a LOVELY time at Brownies," she told Mrs Brightpie. "And guess what – I've got a badge for tying knots. Look!"

She pulled out her vest, so that Mrs Brightpie could see it.

Skirty Marm nudged her again. "Stop flashing your vest! Don't you know it's RUDE to show your underwear at table?" She turned back to Mrs Brightpie. "The other Brownies sew their badges to their uniforms – but they're tiny little human girlies. You can't get Brownie uniforms in witch-sizes."

"What a shame!" cried Mrs Brightpie. "I shall have some specially made for you!"

The witches were thunderstruck. Old Noshie was so thrilled, her mouth dropped open and bits of half-chewed cake fell on the tea-table.

"REAL Brownie uniforms?" she gasped. This was a dream come true. Every time she went to Brownies, Old Noshie longed for a smart yellow shirt and thought how elegant her bald green head would look in the brown hat.

"Of course!" said Mrs Brightpie. "No – don't try to thank me! I'm looking for nice things to do in this village."

After this, Old Noshie and Skirty Marm absolutely loved Mrs Brightpie and thought her one of the very kindest humans they had ever met. And she kept her promise. Two specially made Brownie uniforms arrived at the vicarage three days later, and when Old Noshie put on her brown trousers and yellow shirt, there was no prouder Brownie in the world.

"Such a generous lady!" Mendax said approvingly to the witches. "And so broad-minded." He liked Mrs Brightpie, mainly because she was a new audience for his tall stories. "She was very sympathetic about my terrible war-wound from the Battle of Fungus Gulch. When I described how I begged the doctor to help the others first, she almost wept!"

Skirty Marm rolled her eyes wearily. "For the last time – you weren't at Fungus Gulch. It happened before you were born."

Mendax tossed his head. "Mrs Brightpie says I have a natural talent for storytelling, and she's promised to help me write my memoirs. She says everyone should be encouraged to use their talents."

This piece of wisdom made Skirty Marm very thoughtful. That evening, when the two witches were sitting on their cushions in the belfry, listening to their transistor radio by candlelight, she announced, "Noshie, I've been thinking.

Mrs Brightpie was right. People should be allowed to use their talents."

"Yes," Old Noshie agreed, "I've got a talent for making fizzy drinks come down my nose – but Alice won't let me use it. She says it's RUDE."

Skirty Marm ignored this. "Our talent is for making magic – let's face it, we're not much good at anything else. I think we should use it to give Thomas a proper christening present."

"It's no use," said Old Noshie. "Mr B. says his mind is made up. He'll never let us cast spells on his baby."

"Pooh!" cried Skirty Marm. "Why do we have to tell him? He won't even find out until Thomas learns to talk Hinglish. And then he'll be GRATEFUL."

Old Noshie gasped. This was a very daring and shocking idea. It was one of the naughtiest things Skirty Marm had ever suggested – and she couldn't help liking it.

"If Mr B. was a king in a fairy story," Skirty Marm went on, "instead of a curate, he'd be very glad to have a few good spells at his baby's christening. So we'd really be doing him a favour!"

"Well . . ." Old Noshie said. She loved the idea, but needed to be talked into it. She was not a brave witch and disobeying Mr Babbercorn was a serious matter.

Skirty Marm leapt off her cushion and began to pace up and down across the moonlit floorboards. This was a sure sign that her genius was working furiously.

"It would have to be a very safe present," she said, "and something that didn't show. Put the kettle on, Nosh – let's make a list."

Old Noshie made cups of warm gutter-water, and the two witches settled down with crayons and paper. They discussed and argued and biffed each other all night, until pale dawn crept into the belfry. Finally, they had a list of four possible secret magic gifts to give Thomas:

1. The Gift of never being stuck in a traffic jam.
2. The Gift of making perfect excuses.
3. The Gift of understanding animals.
4. The Gift of twisting long balloons into sausage-dogs.

"Number Four is a load of RUBBISH!" Skirty Marm said scornfully.

Old Noshie stuck out her lip stubbornly. "I

saw a man do it on the vicar's telly. It was brilliant."

"You silly old bat!" Skirty Marm said. "What use will that be to Thomas? Nobody ever became Prime Minister because they could make sausage-dogs out of long balloons! I think we should give him Number One."

"We'd get found out!" shouted Old Noshie. "Alice would GUESS, the minute her car flew over a traffic jam!"

"All right," growled Skirty Marm. "We should go for Number Two – think how useful it'll be when Thomas starts school! He could say the dog ate his homework, and his teachers would believe him!" She sighed heavily. "Trouble is, making excuses is too much like LYING. Mr B. would be very cross with us, and I should hate that."

"Number Three is lovely," Old Noshie said. "Mr B. and Alice might even be pleased. Thomas would be able to talk to the animals, just like Doctor Don'tsmall."

"You mean DR DOLITTLE, you clot!" Skirty Marm biffed Old Noshie to organize her muddled thoughts. "Right then. We'll give Thomas Number Three. It's a tough spell –

but only the best is good enough for our godson!"

The spell was in two parts – a potion and a long poem. Skirty Marm's main job was remembering the poem. It was full of peculiar words in witch-Latin, the ancient language of spells. She and Old Noshie collected the ingredients for the potion. For several nights, they rode around the fields and hedges on their broomsticks, filling their hats with scraps of fur and feathers and bits of insects. They also caught the cries of various animals and stored them in the shell of a hazelnut.

They boiled the potion for three days and three nights until it had bubbled down to a tiny drop, smaller than the head of a pin. Then they took this round to the vicarage and looked for a chance to cast their spell without Mr Babbercorn or Alice seeing (they had both forgotten what a wicked thing they were doing – Skirty Marm said it was fine, because they "meant well").

Their chance came when Alice went to answer the telephone, leaving the witches alone in the vicarage kitchen with Thomas. Quick as a flash, Skirty Marm gabbled the poem, while Old

Noshie dabbed the potion on the bottom of Thomas's little fat foot.

"What are you doing?" Thomas cried, in Babyspeak.

"Don't worry," Old Noshie said. "It's a present for you."

Thomas was teething. He sat in his bouncy chair, chewing the velvet dinosaur from Mrs Brightpie. Suddenly, he threw it across the room and shouted, "I can hear TALKING! There's two beetles having a chat under the floorboards!"

The witches beamed – it had worked.

"I shouldn't think they're having a very interesting conversation," Skirty Marm said, "but you can switch it off if you get bored."

"Listen!" cried Thomas. "I can hear the words the birds are singing outside. This present is WONDERFUL!"

"Don't mention it," Old Noshie said modestly. "But we'd be grateful if you didn't tell your parents – well, you can't yet. But it's a secret."

Alice came back into the room and smiled to see her baby so radiantly happy.

"You two always cheer him up!" she said.

"I'm glad I chose you to be his godmothers."

Skirty Marm and Old Noshie giggled, and nudged each other hard – little did Alice know what brilliant godmothers they really were.

Next morning, Alice met Mrs Brightpie outside the post office.

"Hello, Mrs Brightpie," said Alice. "How are you?"

"Hello, Mrs Babbercorn," said Mrs Brightpie. "I'm extremely well, thank you." She bent over the buggy and smiled her sweet smile at Thomas. "And how is this lovely little boy of yours?"

Thomas was kicking and squawking under his blanket. The tabby cat from the post office sat beside him on the windowsill, staring into his face. When Thomas gave a loud squawk, the cat mewed.

"He's so fond of animals," Alice said fondly. "Anyone would think they were TALKING to each other!"

Mrs Brightpie was thoughtful. There was a moment of silence before she laughed and said she must be getting on.

3

A Disappearance

The peaceful time ended one week before the Harvest Supper. Mr Babbercorn was sitting quietly in the vicarage kitchen, drinking coffee and reading the *Church Times*, when he heard a terrible cry from the study.

He ran in at once – and found the vicar slumped against the desk, his round face almost grey with shock.

"What is it?" gasped Mr Babbercorn. "What on earth has happened?"

He had never seen the plump cheery vicar so upset.

Alice had also heard the terrible cry and came dashing downstairs. Together, she and her husband helped Mr Snelling into a chair.

"It must be my fault . . ." he murmured in a broken voice. "Something I said or did . . ."

There was a sheet of paper crumpled in his

fist. Mr Babbercorn took it and smoothed it out on the desk. He and Alice instantly recognized the neat spiky paw-writing of Mendax.

My Dear Mr Snelling,

By the time you read this, I shall be far away. I have been forced to leave Tranters End – I cannot say why, and it is better for everyone if NOBODY KNOWS WHERE I AM. *Do not try to look for me.*

It breaks my heart to leave you, dear vicar. Before I met you, I had no idea such kindness existed. You took a poor lying cat-slave and showed him the meaning of Goodness. I shall take this with me into my new life – wherever that may be. Think of me sometimes when you eat a jam tart. I shall always be thinking of you,

Your loving sorrowing cat,
       MENDAX

PS I was going to give my little blue cart to the cat at the post office, but I fear he has not the intelligence to use it. Save it for Thomas – and give him a lick from his furry friend M.

PPS This letter does not contain a single LIE.

The letter was in typical flowery Mendax style, but it was splashed with watery blots that looked like tears. Mr Babbercorn and Alice stared at it in dismay.

What would the poor vicar do without his adored talking cat? Who would poach his eggs the way he liked, write his sermons and clean the chocolate-stains off his glasses?

And – the greatest question of all – why had Mendax done this?

"It's nothing to do with you," Alice assured Mr Snelling. "He says he was *forced* to leave – I think something terrible must have happened."

Mr Snelling blew his nose with a forlorn, honking sound that was very moving. "I'd better call PC Bloater – and perhaps if I put a notice in the newspapers and offer a reward—"

Mr Babbercorn shook his head. "Mendax says we mustn't try to look for him. And this isn't a job for the police – I'll fetch Old Noshie and Skirty Marm."

"Yes, this is serious," Skirty Marm said, when she had read the letter several times. "Mendax wouldn't leave this vicarage unless he really, truly had to—" She broke off to pinch Old

35

Noshie's nose. "Stop that grizzling!"

Old Noshie had not been much of a comfort to poor Mr Snelling. The moment she heard that Mendax had run away, she had begun to wail.

"I'm FRIGHTENED!" she wailed now. "This is magic, and we've got the Power Hat so magic isn't supposed to hurt us! Oh, Skirty, perhaps Mrs Abercrombie's horrible SQUASHED GHOST has come out of her tunnel and STOLEN Mendax!"

"Rubbish!" snapped Skirty Marm. "Pull yourself together!" She was stern because she was secretly frightened herself. This was certainly the work of magic – but *who* or *what* could force Mendax to run away, now that Mrs Abercrombie was dead?

"I miss him so much!" sniffed the vicar. "Witches, I can feel that my little cat is in dreadful *danger* – and I must face that danger with him! Don't take any notice of the letter. I want you to cast a finding spell right away!"

Old Noshie and Skirty Marm exchanged uneasy looks. They hated to disappoint Mr Snelling, and they did not want to make him any more worried, but it had to be said.

Skirty Marm spoke as gently as she could.

"It's not as simple as that, I'm afraid. The whole point of the finding spell is to find things that are LOST – and Mendax isn't lost."

"Not lost!" the vicar cried indignantly. "Of course he is! Don't tell me that spell won't work!"

"I quote," said Skirty Marm, "Red-Stocking Spellbook, Chapter two thousand and ninety, page one hundred and eleven thousand. Part A, subsection B. 'Any object that has left a place on purpose, willingly and of its own accord, and then knows where it is when it has got there, SHALL NOT BE DEEMED LOST FOR PURPOSES OF THIS SPELL.'" She added, "I had to write that out two thousand times for a punishment at school."

Mr Snelling's face fell. He did not understand this, but it sounded very legal and definite.

Old Noshie kindly patted his shoulder. "I'm sorry. We'd find him if we could – wouldn't we?"

"Oh, yes," Skirty Marm said. "I haven't always seen eye to eye with that cat, but it won't be the same village without him."

"I'll make you a nice cup of tea," said Alice. "Then you can have a rest, to get over the shock. Cuthbert and I will carry on arranging the Harvest Supper."

Mr Snelling shook his head forlornly and stood up. "Mendax wouldn't want me to mope. He'd expect me to carry on. I don't want to let him down."

The vicar was as good as his word and went on with his work in the same old way. But his unhappy face made everyone very sad.

In a few hours, the news that Mendax had left was all round the village. The people of Tranters End were sorry to lose the little talking cat – but they were even sorrier for their vicar.

The next day was a Sunday. The villagers came to church as usual. It seemed very empty without the familiar figure of Mendax bustling about. Normally he was sitting on the pile of hymnbooks at the door, ready to chat to people as they came in. It was hard to look at his empty cushion, though everyone tried to be cheerful for poor Mr Snelling's sake.

Mendax usually took the collection, carrying the plate carefully between his paws. Today, Mr Noggs the churchwarden carried the plate instead, and several people sniffed as they dropped in their money.

Thomas would not lie quietly in his buggy. He moaned, "Where's Mendax? He promised to tell me a story!" Alice tried picking him up and rocking him in her arms, but still he shouted, in Babyspeak, "I want Mendax!"

When it came to the sermon, Mr Snelling plodded up the pulpit steps as if he had the world on his shoulders.

"You will all know by now," he said, in a choking voice, "that I have lost my little cat. I didn't have the heart to write my own sermon – and they're very boring, anyway. So I've brought Mendax's classic one about the Good Samaritan."

He read it out very shakily and nearly broke

down twice. Altogether, it was a sad service. Afterwards, everyone tried to think of something comforting to say to the vicar.

Mrs Brightpie patted his arm gently. "Now, Mr Snelling, you're not to fret. Mendax is a very clever cat. I'm sure he can take care of himself. And cats aren't like us humans, you know – they don't feel things as deeply."

"Mendax does," Mr Snelling said. "He has the kindest heart in the world!"

"You mustn't lose hope," soothed Mrs Brightpie. "Why, he might come strolling back any minute!"

"I wish he would!" sniffed Old Noshie as she followed Skirty Marm back up the one hundred and eighty-six steps to the belfry. "Oh, Skirt, nothing's right without Mendax!"

Skirty Marm had been frowning a lot ever since she had read Mendax's letter. It was her thinking frown, which showed her clever brain was working hard.

"I just wish I knew what made him so scared that he had to run away! If it is something to do with magic, why didn't he leave a message for us?"

4

The Warning of the Ants

Mr Babbercorn had suggested cancelling the Harvest Supper because of Mendax's disappearance. The vicar, however, would not hear of it.

"Mendax did a lot of work for this Harvest Supper – why, he left a bag of sponge cakes in the freezer specially! If we didn't have it, we'd be letting him down."

Mrs Brightpie said the vicar was very brave. And despite having a bad leg and not being very strong, she insisted on helping with the arrangements. Thanks to her, the Harvest Supper was a splendid affair. Sad as they were about Mendax, the people of Tranters End could not help gasping with delight when they filed into the village hall.

"Wow!" cried Old Noshie. "Look at the GRUB!"

Mrs Brightpie had tried to cheer things up by decorating the hall with branches of apples, bunches of grapes and coloured paper lanterns. The long tables were groaning with food. As well as the things the villagers had given, Mrs Brightpie had paid for huge bowls of delicious trifle, jellies in every colour of the rainbow and plates of sweets for the children.

"Bless her!" whispered Alice, with tears in her eyes. "She won't let us miss him too much!"

It was hard not to have a good time when Mrs Brightpie herself sat down at the piano and played country dances. Old Noshie and Skirty Marm loved to dance, and they jumped and pranced like two whirling dervishes. They were wearing their new Brownie uniforms in public for the first time, which greatly added to their enjoyment.

"If only Mendax hadn't run away," Skirty Marm said, "this would be PERFECT!"

Thomas was still cross and grizzly. Alice had parked his buggy in the little kitchen that opened off the hall, but this only made him worse. About halfway through the supper he broke into roars, and Alice had to shut the door so nobody would hear him. She rocked him and jiggled him and sang his favourite songs. And still he bellowed.

The music was loud, and the witches did not hear Thomas until they stopped for a rest. Skirty Marm, who had very sharp ears, suddenly grabbed Old Noshie by the sleeve of her Brownie shirt.

"Listen! He's calling US!"

Sure enough, over the jolly strains of "Strip the Willow", they heard Thomas's voice: "Noshie! Skirty! HELP!"

They rushed out to the kitchen.

"AT LAST!" yelled Thomas, in Babyspeak. And he stopped crying.

"Thank goodness!" gasped Alice. "I don't know what's the matter with him tonight!"

"Send her away," ordered Thomas. "I have to talk to you *in private*!"

The witches knew there was no point saying this to Alice – she still refused to believe that they could understand her baby.

"Poor Alice, you haven't had any supper," said Skirty Marm. "You go and have something to eat – we'll take care of Thomas."

Alice was rather puzzled, but too relieved to

get away from her squealing baby to ask any questions.

"Thanks, witches. I'll only be a minute." She paused on her way out of the kitchen. "This place is full of ants, and they keep trying to climb on the buggy. Do keep them away from Thomas."

The damp little kitchen was swarming with tiny black ants. A line of them were marching up the handle of Thomas's buggy.

"Shoo!" said Old Noshie. "Pesky things!" She had brought a plate of flapjacks and did not intend to share them with a lot of greedy ants.

"Leave them alone!" cried Thomas. "They've come with a WARNING!"

Skirty Marm sat down beside him. "All right, what's all this about?"

"It's Mrs Brightpie!" Thomas said. "You have to make her go away!"

"Go away? Certainly not!" said Skirty Marm. "She's turned this Harvest Supper into the brilliantest party ever – and she got us these smart Brownie uniforms!"

"She said I was the best dancer in the village," Old Noshie added proudly.

"You don't understand!" moaned Thomas.

"The ants told me she's DANGEROUS and HORRIBLE!"

Old Noshie and Skirty Marm burst out laughing.

"What, Mrs Brightpie?" Old Noshie took a big bite of her flapjack, which the kind lady had provided. "She's a WONDERFUL human!"

"She's a WITCH!" Thomas cried. "The ants recognized her!"

Skirty Marm looked sternly at the ants. "What do they know about anything? And what have they got against witches? They'll be telling US to go away next!"

"Cheek!" said Old Noshie, with her mouth full.

Skirty Marm patted Thomas's velvety bald head. "Now, Thomas," she said, in a kind-but-firm voice copied from Mr Babbercorn, "when we gave you that lovely present, we didn't expect you to believe any old rubbish the animals told you! Ants are well-known troublemakers. They'll do anything to get at human food."

The ants began to mill about on the buggy and on the floor, as if they were angry.

"They're just jealous of our lovely party," Old

Noshie said comfortably. "Back home on Witch Island, we eat ants."

"Don't you eat any of these!" Thomas screamed, kicking his short legs furiously. "They're my FRIENDS!"

"Keep your hair on," said Skirty Marm. "I mean, keep your fuzz on. This sort of thing is typical ant behaviour. You're very tired from all that yelling, so I'm going to cast one of my sleep spells. And you're not to worry."

She muttered her sleep spell. Thomas, in the middle of his fury, suddenly yawned and smiled. Before Skirty had finished, he was fast asleep.

"You'll be in trouble, if Alice finds out about that spell," said Old Noshie. "Cor, doesn't he make a lot of noise for such a little person?"

"What a load of old RUBBISH about Mrs Brightpie!" exclaimed Skirty Marm. She stamped her foot crossly at the scurrying ants. "Get out of this kitchen!"

At that moment, the door opened and in came Mrs Brightpie herself. She was carrying a tray of dirty plates, and she gave the witches one of her sweet smiles. It was very hard indeed to believe that this kind lady – who had given them their treasured Brownie uniforms – was wicked or dangerous.

"You clever things, you've got poor little Thomas off to sleep!" she said. "I wonder what was the matter with him?"

Old Noshie happened to be standing beside the sink, which was full of water. In the second before Mrs Brightpie dropped in the plates, Old Noshie saw something reflected on the smooth surface of the water – something that turned her green skin the colour of a raw sprout.

Where she should have seen the pretty face of Mrs Brightpie, she saw a hideous, HAIRY FACE. Where she should have seen Mrs Brightpie's charming smile, she saw a deadly row of METAL TEETH.

It was the face that haunted her worst nightmares – the kind of nightmares she got after eating human cheese, which never agreed with her.

She stood with her mouth hanging open and her eyes like saucers.

"What's up with you?" asked Skirty Marm after Mrs Brightpie had left the kitchen.

At first, Old Noshie could only make a strange grunting noise. "Huuurrrrr . . ."

Skirty Marm took off her friend's pointed hat and blue wig, and gave her bald head a brisk whack with a teacup.

"It's for your own good, Nosh. Now tell me what's the matter – you look like you've seen a ghost!"

"I HAVE!" croaked Old Noshie. "I saw MRS ABERCROMBIE! It was meant to be Mrs Brightpie's reflection – but it was HERS!"

Skirty Marm was frightened. "Don't YOU start!" she yelled.

"I did, Skirt – honest I did! And you know what that means!"

"When a witch wants to disguise herself," Skirty Marm said, "she can take on any shape – but she can't disguise her REFLECTION. Of course I know that – it was one of our first lessons! But Mrs Brightpie's not like that. She's not evil or ugly – and anyway, someone would have noticed by now. How could she go to the hairdressers if she couldn't show her reflection?"

There was a terrible chilly feeling in the pit of Skirty Marm's stomach. She knew Old Noshie was telling the truth, but she still did not want to believe it.

"Anyway, that's not a proper reflection," she blustered. "That's just scummy washing-up water! Let's get back into the hall and look at her proper reflection in a window or something. Then you'll see this is STUPID!"

"I don't dare," quavered Old Noshie. "Oh, Skirty, what are we going to do? She didn't die in that tunnel after all! And now she's come here to snatch back the Power Hat – and we'll be KILLED!"

Before Skirty Marm could reply, Alice came back into the kitchen. "Oh, how wonderful – Thomas is asleep! Thank you for looking after him, witches."

She was slightly surprised when Skirty Marm grabbed Old Noshie by the arm and dragged her out of the room without a word.

In the hall, the Harvest Supper was in full swing. The village children played games under the long tables, eating the sweets Mrs Brightpie had given them. The grown-ups sat with cups of tea or danced to the loud music that boomed from Mrs Tucker's tape-deck.

Mrs Brightpie could not dance because of her bad leg. She sat beside the vicar, and you could see from the expression on her face that she was saying comforting things about Mendax. It really was extremely difficult to believe that this kind lady had anything to do with the dreadful Mrs Abercrombie.

Skirty Marm heaved a shaky sigh of relief. "You really got me going that time, you old IDIOT!" she snapped. "We'll find her reflection, and then you'll see that you're BONKERS!"

She looked around the hall, so beautifully decorated for the Harvest Supper – and saw that every single window had been covered with sheaves of corn or huge bunches of leaves. Not a single thing on any of the tables was shiny enough to reflect anything. Even the spoons were made of dull white plastic.

Skirty Marm breathed gently on the palm of her hand, and her lips moved with the words of a spell. Her palm began to shine as if someone had covered it with a sheet of mercury. Very quickly, making super-sure nobody but Noshie was watching, she tilted her gleaming silver palm towards Mrs Brightpie.

"Told you," muttered Old Noshie.

Skirty Marm could not speak. Across the room, Mrs Brightpie sat with her hand on Mr Snelling's knee. In the reflection, the innocent vicar was sitting next to the evil ugly figure of Mrs Abercrombie.

5

True Colours

At the end of the Harvest Supper, Mr Snelling made a speech thanking Mrs Brightpie for all her generosity. She stood beside the door, shaking hands with every single person as they left.

To Mr Babbercorn's annoyance, Old Noshie and Skirty Marm refused to line up for the hand-shaking. They had started to behave very oddly – whispering and trembling and trying to hide behind the hall curtains.

"I really think you should come and thank Mrs Brightpie," Mr Babbercorn told them.

"NO!" squealed the witches.

They jumped up to the ceiling like two enormous frogs, and wriggled out through the skylight.

"I'm terribly sorry," Mr Babbercorn said to Mrs Brightpie. "I can't think why they're being so rude."

"Don't worry!" laughed Mrs Brightpie, warmly shaking his hand, "Witches will be witches!"

Back at the vicarage, the increasingly exasperated curate found Old Noshie and Skirty Marm crouching under the draining-board with tea towels over their faces.

"For goodness sake!" Mr Babbercorn said, rather sharply. "What has got into you two? Why on earth did you zoom out through the roof like that?"

"Don't be too hard on them," said gentle Alice. "I think something has frightened them. Come out, witches – there's nothing to be scared of here!"

"Draw the blinds!" hissed Skirty Marm, behind her tea towel.

Mr Babbercorn and Mr Snelling sighed impatiently, but Alice drew the blinds across the kitchen windows. Only then did the witches dare to uncover their faces and crawl out.

"I've had a terrible SHOCK!" moaned Old Noshie. "I need a HUGE BISCUIT!"

"You'd better sit down, you lot," Skirty Marm said grimly. "We've got some bad news."

Pale and trembling, she told them the awful truth – that the lady they knew as Mrs Brightpie was Mrs Abercrombie in disguise.

For a long moment, there was a stunned silence. Then the three grown-up humans burst out *laughing* – even Mr Snelling, who had not so much as smiled since the disappearance of Mendax. They laughed and laughed. The bare idea of delightful Mrs Brightpie secretly being the evil Mrs Abercrombie was too hilarious for words.

"Oh, you ridiculous witches!" cried Mr Snelling. "What will you think of next?"

"They don't believe us!" wailed Old Noshie.

Skirty Marm stamped her foot. "You fools!" she shouted. "Why won't you listen to us? Don't you care that we're in DANGER?"

Mr Babbercorn wiped the tears of laughter from his glasses.

"Of course we care," he said. "But you're not in danger! Mrs Brightpie wouldn't hurt a fly!"

"No – she'd be too busy EATING them!" growled Skirty Marm.

"We've seen Mrs Abercrombie, so we know what she looks like," Mr Snelling pointed out. He shuddered. "She's huge and hideous – and dear Mrs Brightpie is very nice-looking, I always think." He cleared his throat and blushed slightly. "She told me her first name is 'Petunia'. I think it suits her."

"It's all a trick!" Skirty Marm raged. "She had us fooled too! She was asking us very sneaky questions about the Power Hat – thank goodness we didn't tell her where it was!"

"Or we'd be DEAD," Old Noshie put in solemnly.

"I tell you, that woman is a desperate witch!" cried Skirty Marm. "We have to BURN her immediately!"

"Oh, do be reasonable," sighed Mr Snelling. "How can we burn a respectable lady like Mrs Brightpie? This is nonsense!"

"You're just over-excited," Alice said kindly. "When you've had a good night's sleep, you'll realize you're being silly."

"Don't you see?" Skirty Marm cried. "This must be why Mendax ran away! He must have seen her reflection in something and lost his nerve!"

The mention of Mendax made everyone very serious.

"My Mendax is not a coward," Mr Snelling said proudly. "He'd never run away because he was scared. Really, witches – let's have an end to this at once! I won't have poor Mrs Brightpie insulted! Certainly not when she's given all that money to the organ fund."

Skirty Marm spoke bitterly. "Yes, she BOUGHT you. Just like she BOUGHT me and Nosh with these Brownie uniforms. Come on, Noshie. Let's go home and take them off!"

The two witches left the vicarage without saying goodnight. They climbed up the one hundred and eighty-six belfry steps and changed back into their witchy rags. Then Skirty Marm dragged her cushion over to her favourite thinking place, under the larger of the two great bells.

Old Noshie plumped down beside her. "What do we do now, Skirt?" she asked in a small, worried voice.

"Nothing," said Skirty Marm grimly, "except WAIT. She'll reveal herself to us when she's ready. And I mean to be ready too!"

Deep in the woods, hidden by a thick grove of trees, a light burned in the window of Mrs Brightpie's cottage. The people of Tranters End – who had had such a splendid time at the Harvest Supper – would have been astonished at the scene in the kitchen.

An iron cauldron was bubbling over a large fire. Mrs Brightpie, no longer smiling, was pacing up and down impatiently. A rusty iron cage hung beside the window. Inside it was the huddled form of Mendax. He did not look sleek or elegant now. One of his ears was bent, his whiskers drooped and he was shaking like a leaf.

His green eyes were fixed fearfully on the third creature in the room. At the table sat a very dirty old witch, with only one black tooth and filthy grey hair. She was chewing her way through a huge plate of deep-fried mice (and very horrible it sounded when she crunched them in her gums). Every now and then, this toothless old witch took a swig from a large brown bottle of Nasty Medicine. As all sensible humans know, it is very STUPID and DANGEROUS to drink someone else's medicine, but witches regard it as a treat.

And this old witch certainly loved it. Mendax shuddered as he remembered her drunken rages. Seeing her was like seeing his worst nightmare for she was none other than Mrs Wilkins, the coarse and low-class witch who had once owned him. And although the cat-slaves were now free, Mrs Wilkins still had power over him – because she knew his code.

I should explain that, in the bad old days, every cat-slave had a code (rather like the number on a credit card) known only to his owner. This meant that no cat could have a secret – his owner could always activate the code and get it out of him. Mendax had run away from the vicarage when he spotted Mrs Brightpie's horrible reflection in a puddle and realized that if she got his code he would not be able to help giving away the secret of the Power Hat. He hadn't had time to warn the witches.

"Get on with it!" shouted Mrs Brightpie crossly. "I warn you, Mrs Wilkins – my patience is running out!"

"I'm still hungry," mumbled Mrs Wilkins. "They starved us in that prison. And I sold all me teeth to buy Medicine, so eating takes me a while these days."

After the defeat of the queen, Mrs Wilkins had done a stretch in prison for cruelty to cat-slaves.

"Hurry up!" snapped Mrs Brightpie. She whacked Mendax's cage with her stick. "I'm paying you for this cat's CODE! Once I've got it, he'll have to tell me where they hid my Power Hat!"

"Using cat-codes is against the law on Witch Island now," said Mrs Wilkins. "If I get found out, I'll go straight back to prison. You'd better kill him when you've finished, in case he reports us."

"Mind your own business!" stormed the former queen. "And finish that food! I want my Power Hat before morning – and before those two interfering Red-Stockings find out I've got Mendax!"

"Good thing you caught him so quickly," Mrs Wilkins remarked. A mouse's tail hung from her lower lip. She sucked it in like a strand of spaghetti. "You want to watch him. He's *slippery*, that one."

"He won't be able to lie when you've given me his code," said Mrs Brightpie.

Inside the cage, Mendax groaned.

Mrs Brightpie ignored the heart-rending sound. "This human disguise is very hard work," she said. "While you're guzzling, I'll change into something more comfortable."

Before the horrified eyes of Mendax, her pretty white curls changed to greasy snakes of grey. Her teeth turned to metal. A rough beard sprouted on her chin. She swelled and grew until her head brushed the ceiling. Her neat blue dress changed to musty, dusty black rags.

Mrs Abercrombie, ex-queen of Witch Island, was herself again. The sight was so ugly that Mendax had to stuff a paw in his mouth to hold back a scream.

"Cor, that's better!" said Mrs Wilkins. "You didn't half look sickening in that disguise!"

Her plate was nearly empty. Mendax had served her many meals in the miserable past and recognized the signs that she was getting tired of eating. Any minute now, his secrets would be torn from him like a cork being pulled out of a bottle.

"Mrs Abercrombie will grab the Power Hat and make it do UNSPEAKABLE things," Mendax whispered sadly to himself. "Noshie and Skirty will be killed – I'll probably end up in some illegal Cat Pie—"

He stopped suddenly. A small brown spider was scurrying across the windowsill beside him. Mendax remembered the magic christening gift.

Without moving a whisker he whispered, "Listen, spider – this is an EMERGENCY! Get a message to the baby at the vicarage. Tell him to tell the witches – SAVE THE HAT!"

Old Noshie and Skirty Marm had fallen asleep on the belfry floor – Old Noshie pointlessly clutching a brick to use as a weapon in case Mrs Abercrombie appeared. At the dead of night, when the moon was high and the village was cloaked in darkness, they were woken up by the screams of Thomas. Distantly, they heard him yelling.

"Witches – message from Mendax! Come quickly!"

Skirty Marm was the first to wake up properly. She leapt to her feet.

"Come on, Nosh – Thomas wants us!"

Old Noshie scrambled up, rubbing her sleepy eyes, and dropped the brick on her foot. "OW!"

The two of them rushed down the one hundred and eighty-six belfry steps and hurried across the dark garden to the vicarage. There, they found the vicar, Mr Babbercorn and Alice desperately trying to comfort a shrieking baby.

Alice was almost crying. "Oh witches, can

you do anything? He's been screaming for hours, and I don't know what's the matter!"

"ABOUT TIME!" yelled Thomas, in Babyspeak.

"Sorry, Thomas," said Old Noshie. "What's the message?"

"Mrs Abercrombie has got Mendax!" Thomas cried. "He says SAVE THE HAT before she breaks his code!"

"Who told you?" demanded Skirty Marm. "Are you sure it's not one of his lies?"

"Mendax told a spider, who told a bird," Thomas said. "The bird tapped his beak on the window and told me. And I had to scream until you heard."

"Nice work!" said Old Noshie, patting his bald head. "You can go back to sleep now."

And to the amazement of his exhausted parents, Thomas fell asleep. It was as if someone had switched off a radio.

"I don't understand!" said Alice when they were all standing in the kitchen. "What is going on?"

"Ummm . . ." said Old Noshie.

"Err . . ." said Skirty Marm.

They didn't dare tell Mr Babbercorn and Alice

that they had been casting spells on the baby. They knew Mr Babbercorn would be very cross with them. Skirty Marm gave Old Noshie a hard stare which meant, "Shut up and leave this to me".

"If you understood Babyspeak," she said slowly, "you'd know that Mrs Brightpie—"

"Right, that's enough!" interrupted Mr Babbercorn. It was the middle of the night, and he was very tired. This made him less patient than usual. "I don't want to hear *one more word* about poor Mrs Brightpie being Mrs Abercrombie in disguise. Mrs Abercrombie is dead. This is a lot of NONSENSE!"

"She's not dead!" cried Old Noshie. "We've got to get the— OW!"

Skirty Marm had cut her off by slapping her with a tea towel. "You'll be sorry you didn't believe us," she said darkly. "Come on, Nosh – let's not waste any more time with these silly humans!"

She grabbed Old Noshie by her ragged dress and pulled her out through the back door.

"You're barmy!" grumbled Old Noshie, out in the dark vicarage garden. "Why didn't you fetch the Power Hat?"

"Mr B. wouldn't have let us," snapped Skirty Marm. "We'll have to SNEAK it away, without him knowing."

"But HOW, Skirt?"

The Power Hat, disguised as a knitted bobble hat, was hidden in Mr Babbercorn's underwear drawer. This was the safe place they had chosen for it the last time Mrs Abercrombie had tried to steal it back. Mr Babbercorn had almost forgotten it was there – though it kept his vests and pants in such perfect condition that they never wore out.

Skirty Marm was scornful. "You really are a very THICK WITCH, Noshie. Don't you remember the spell we learned at school, in the 37th form?"

"I've forgotten," Old Noshie said. "I must have been eating my packed lunch."

"We're going to make ourselves INVISIBLE," Skirty Marm said sternly. "Put your wig on straight and repeat after me . . ."

Skirty Marm had a very good memory, but she did not have her Red-Stocking Spellbook. When the Invisibility Spell was complete, both witches shrieked. They had disappeared – but their clothes had not. The invisible Old Noshie looked especially strange, with her pointed hat and lopsided blue wig hanging in mid-air above her ragged dress.

"Drat," muttered Skirty Marm. "I must have left something out!"

"Let's try again," suggested Old Noshie.

Skirty Marm shook her head – her friend could tell by the way her empty hat wobbled in the air. "There's no time. Mrs A. could be here any minute to grab the hat! Don't you see? Mendax sent the message because he knew Mrs A. had his CODE! We'll just have to take all our clothes off."

"What?" gasped Old Noshie. "And go creeping round the vicarage IN THE NUDE? Are you MAD?"

Skirty Marm's clothes were already dropping in a crumpled heap on the lawn. "They won't be able to SEE us – that's the whole point! Now, hurry up and take your clothes off."

Old Noshie did not like it, but she always did as she was told in the end. Her clothes joined the heap. Both witches were now totally invisible.

"BRRR!" grumbled the voice of Old Noshie, eerie in the darkness. "I've got goose-pimples the size of acorns!"

"Shhh!" hissed the voice of Skirty Marm.

"Where are you, Skirt?"

"In the bushes." Skirty Marm rustled the laurel bushes to show Old Noshie where she was.

In chilly, naked silence, the two witches waited for the lights to go out in the vicarage. When the house was dark and quiet, they tiptoed across the lawn.

"Hang on – what's this?" Skirty Marm snatched at a strange shape bobbing through the air beside her. "You old fool – you forgot to take off your WIG!"

"Give it back, smelly!" growled Old Noshie. "It's all right for you – you've got HAIR! My head's freezing!"

Skirty Marm threw the blue wig across the garden. Old Noshie tried to smack Skirty Marm, but could not find her. She spat on Skirty's clothes instead. Skirty Marm squashed Old Noshie's pointed hat.

"This is stupid!" she whispered crossly. "We haven't got time to fight! The minute she gets that cat's code, we're sunk!"

"All right," muttered Old Noshie. "I'll biff you when I can see you."

The invisible witches climbed into the vicarage through the bathroom window. They crept into the hall – and got a shock when they came face to face with their nude reflections in the big mirror (very few spells can fool a mirror).

Somewhere above them, they could hear the snores of Mr Snelling. They scurried up the stairs. Very careful not to tread on any creaking floorboards, they tiptoed into the curate's bedroom.

Mr Babbercorn and Alice lay fast asleep in the big double bed. Thomas lay fast asleep in his cot. Slowly – a centimetre at a time – the witches pulled open the drawer where Mr Babbercorn kept his underwear.

Skirty Marm rummaged inside it and whisked out the Power Hat in its disguise as a black-and-white bobble hat. She rammed it on her invisible head. She had worn the Power Hat before and did not enjoy it. The Hat did not weigh much when you held it in your hand, but it lay upon the brain like a ton of lead.

As long as Skirty Marm was wearing it, however, the witches were safe. Their teeth chattering with cold, they left the house, picked

up their clothes from the garden and rushed up the one hundred and eighty-six steps to the belfry. Skirty Marm reversed the spell to make them visible again, and they heaved deep sighs of relief as they scrambled into their clothes. Old Noshie, who hated being invisible, kept looking affectionately at her hands and trying to squint over her shoulder to check that her bottom was still there.

"Mrs A. can't hurt us now!" she said.

"Maybe not!" snarled a terrible voice. "But I can hurt MENDAX!"

There was a blinding flash of lightning, and the witches screamed in terror. Mrs Abercrombie, her metal teeth gleaming wickedly, was in their belfry.

6

The Helpful Hat

"I've been PATIENT!" roared Mrs Abercrombie. "I've watched you two, waiting for you to lead me to the Hat! And I was TOO LATE! Drat and double-drat! By the time that cat told me where it was, there was nothing in the drawer but UNDERWEAR! So it's time to face you IN PERSON!"

Old Noshie bravely picked up her brick and hurled it at Mrs Abercrombie's face. The former queen caught it in her mouth, crunched it up like a gingernut and swallowed it. Then she licked her lips and smiled horribly.

"I've been looking forward to this – I bet you're THRILLED to see me!"

Skirty Marm stood up as straight as she could and folded her arms to hide their trembling.

"We've been expecting you," she said. "And you're wasting your time. The Power Hat is on my head – and that's where it's STAYING."

Mrs Abercrombie's sudden scowl of fury was a terrible thing to see. Old Noshie ran behind Skirty Marm and peeped over her shoulder.

"I missed it!" Mrs Abercrombie shrieked. "It was nearly in my grasp – and I missed it! I'd like to know how that blasted little cat-slave managed to warn you! But it's not over yet. Your queen has come with an offer."

"You're not our queen!" shouted Skirty Marm. She stuck out her tongue, which was dark purple. "What can you do to us? POOH to your offer – and shut the door on your way out."

"Miserable Red-Stocking!" thundered the ex-queen. "Give me my Power Hat!"

"NO!" yelled Skirty Marm.

"No!" squeaked Old Noshie.

Mrs Abercrombie looked around for something to sit on. There were no chairs in the belfry, so she picked up the witches' cushions and settled herself on the floor with a loud grunt.

"Let's be reasonable," she said. "You don't know how to use my Hat. It's wasted on you. You don't understand what I've been through to

72

get my hands on it. I used my underground cave on Witch Island to make myself piles of rubbishy human money. And when I'd made enough, I blew up the cave and let everyone think I was dead. Then I came here and had to pretend to be nice to humans. It's been very hard work."

"I suppose the State Funeral's off now," Old Noshie said, in a disappointed voice. "I was looking forward to the fireworks."

Mrs Abercrombie ignored this. Her mean little eyes stared hard at Skirty Marm. "Here's my offer. Give me back my Power Hat, and I'll allow you to live. What's more, I'll allow that skinny little cat to live too."

"If I give you the Hat, you'll destroy the peaceful, democratic government of Witch Island," said Skirty Marm. "You'll kill or imprison every witch who stands against you!"

"True," said Mrs Abercrombie. "But why should you care about that? You can stay here. We don't want your sort on Witch Island anyway – you and your filthy human ways!"

"We care about Chancellor Badsleeves and all our friends," said Skirty Marm sternly. "We'll never let you hurt them!"

"Well, that's just the sort of thing I mean," said Mrs Abercrombie. "Filthy." A shudder of disgust rippled across her huge body.

Old Noshie whispered in Skirty Marm's ear, "Ask her what will happen if we DON'T give her the Hat!"

"Your daft green pal shows a glimmer of sense for once," Mrs Abercrombie said, with a spine-chilling cackle. "What a good question! If you DON'T give me my Hat, I will EAT the cat-slave Mendax. It's your choice."

The witches stared at each other in dismay. This looked impossible. If Mrs Abercrombie ate Mendax poor Mr Snelling's heart would break.

But if they saved Mendax, by giving the Hat to Mrs Abercrombie, their friends on Witch Island would have a terrible time. Chancellor Badsleeves and her Red-Stocking government would be killed immediately, probably in some particularly horrible new way. Mrs Abercrombie was famous for thinking up new ways to kill other witches – she had written a classic book on the subject (*A Hundred Horrible Deaths*, published by Belch & Squelch at 10 Witch-shillings, please allow 28 years for delivery).

"Oh, Skirt!" quavered Old Noshie. "Whatever shall we do?"

Skirty Marm suddenly remembered she was wearing the Power Hat. She shut her eyes, and spoke to it inside her head, so Mrs Abercrombie would not hear her. "Hat – Mrs A.'s right – I don't know enough about you to use you properly. Can't you just tell me if there's anything I can do?"

Green letters appeared on the blackness inside her head – rather like the letters on an old-fashioned computer screen.

I'm not supposed to give advice, typed the Hat.

Skirty Marm sighed impatiently. "You've become a very SOPPY Hat since you turned Good! Can't you just give me a *clue*?"

I am not permitted to express political opinions, typed the Hat. *But you are right, incompetent and ignorant witch – I do hate Mrs Abercrombie and I dread doing her dirty work again! So pay attention. I shall type this only once. You must command me to give Mendax a good CLOAKING.*

"A *what*?" Skirty Marm asked, in her thoughts.

It means I cloak him in a shell of protective magic, typed the Power Hat. *She can keep the cat, but she won't be able to eat him – she won't be able to hurt him at all.*

"Just the thing!" cried Skirty, inwardly. "Hat – give Mendax a cloaking!"

Certainly. But there's a slight snag, typed the Hat. *It only lasts for one week, and it cannot be renewed. So you will have just one week to rescue your cat-friend. After that, he will be cat-fritters.*

Mrs Abercrombie suddenly leapt up and stamped her foot so hard that one of the floorboards cracked.

"Something's been CLOAKED!" she screamed, turning puce with fury. "I can feel it! Drat and double-drat – you've cloaked that pesky cat!"

"What's she talking about?" wondered Old Noshie.

"Shut your green face!" roared Mrs Abercrombie. She turned back to Skirty Marm, simmering with rage. "So – you think you're clever because you know about Advanced Cloaking! But the fight isn't over yet! This time next week, you'll be begging me ON YOUR

KNEES to take the Power Hat!"

She raised her arms – and vanished.

Her voice hung in the empty air: "Remember – one week!"

The witches were very pleased and proud to have got rid of Mrs Abercrombie, but the pleasure wore off when they realized they were no nearer to saving Mendax.

"This cloaking thing isn't much use if Mrs A.'s still got him!" sighed Old Noshie. "And we've only got a week to think of something!"

It was all the harder because their friends at the vicarage would not hear a word against Mrs Brightpie. They did not believe the witches' garbled story about cloaking Mendax in magic. They were all getting very annoyed with Old Noshie and Skirty Marm.

"For the last time," Mr Snelling said crossly, "I don't want to hear any more about Mrs Brightpie being wicked. I don't want to hear how she's got my Mendax – why, she's put a notice about him in the post office window, offering a reward to anyone who sees him! Don't tell me the late Mrs Abercrombie ever did anything as nice as that!"

Mr Babbercorn tried to be kind and

understanding. "Perhaps you're a bit jealous of Mrs Brightpie," he suggested, "because everyone likes her so much."

"JEALOUS?" gasped the witches. This was so unfair it was absolutely outrageous. It was particularly awful to be thought nasty and selfish when they were trying so hard to be brave and good.

One by one, the days slipped past. Old Noshie and Skirty Marm stayed miserably in their belfry, racking their brains for a way of saving Mendax before the cloaking spell ran out.

For this reason, they did not hear of Mrs Brightpie's latest plan – until it was too late.

The last day of the cloaking spell was Hallowe'en. For witches this is the most important night of the year, when they ride out on their broomsticks to play tricks on innocent humans. For humans, however, Hallowe'en means nothing more than fun – and the people of Tranters End were delighted when Mrs Brightpie invited every child in the village to a grand party at her new house in the woods.

"My house is full of surprises!" smiled Mrs

Brightpie. "I'd like the dear children to see it first!"

"How kind," Alice said when she heard about the party. "I wish Thomas was big enough to go – it's bound to be wonderful."

At teatime on Hallowe'en, the twenty children of Tranters End set out through the woods. They were wearing Hallowe'en costumes – the three Blenkinsops, from Blodge Farm, were particularly gruesome as vampires, with false blood dripping out of their mouths. Little Amy Noggs, dressed as a red demon with plastic horns, carried a large bunch of flowers for Mrs Brightpie. All the children were very excited and very curious to see what Mrs Brightpie had done to the woodman's cottage.

"WOW!" cried Ben Blenkinsop.

The children gaped at the cottage, sitting so prettily in its sunlit clearing.

Its walls were reddish-brown and looked soft to the touch. Emma Blenkinsop prodded it with her finger – and shrieked when her finger sank in. It looked soft because it was soft. It was soft because it was made of moist, delicious slabs of *gingerbread*.

The windows were surrounded with white

chocolate. The front door was made of dark chocolate and surrounded with a pretty pattern of Maltesers. The sloping roof was covered with green and red fruit gums. The window boxes were made of toffee and filled with liquorice-allsort flowers.

With yells of hungry delight, the children rushed up to the house and began pulling bits off.

Only Amy Noggs hung back. She watched the others stuffing themselves with cake, sweets and toffee.

"Only WICKED WITCHES have ginger-bread houses!" she whispered.

Nobody heard her.

7

Panic

It was nearly dark when the parents of Tranters End trooped through the woods to collect their children from Mrs Brightpie's Hallowe'en party. They were all impatient to get a look at her famous cottage.

"I've heard she's put in a swimming pool," said Mrs Blenkinsop.

"No, no!" said Mr Noggs the churchwarden, who was Amy's grandfather. "She's built a huge conservatory!"

"Here we are," said Mrs Tucker, who was fetching her two young nephews. "Well – doesn't it look a picture?"

Deep in the forest, the grey stone walls of the cottage glowed in the last rays of the setting sun. It was as neat and quaint as a picture on a calendar with its red-tiled roof and window boxes full of geraniums.

The parents were a little distance away but they could see the dainty figure of Mrs Brightpie, waiting for them in the cottage doorway.

"Isn't it quiet?" remarked Mrs Blenkinsop. "You'd never think there was a children's party going on, would you?" She sounded uneasy. "You wouldn't catch me living out here in the middle of nowhere!"

They hurried towards Mrs Brightpie. By now, the silence seemed decidedly strange.

"Good evening, Mrs Brightpie," said Mr Noggs. "I hope the kids haven't worn you out!"

"Not at all!" smiled Mrs Brightpie.

The parents stood listening to the wind in the trees and the deepening silence. Mrs Brightpie watched them, still smiling.

After a few minutes, Mrs Tucker cleared her throat nervously.

"Where – where *are* the children?"

"I've got your children," said Mrs Brightpie.

And before their horrified eyes, a terrible change swept over her. She grew until she filled the doorway. Her eyes glinted fiendishly. Her teeth became metal daggers, and suddenly she wore the tattered black rags of a WITCH.

Several of the parents screamed. They all

knew at once that this was not a witch like Old Noshie and Skirty Marm, but a wicked witch from a nightmare.

Mr Noggs tried to sound brave.

"Give us the children and we'll say no more about this."

Mrs Abercrombie chortled. There was a flash of lightning and a mighty clap of thunder. Mrs Blenkinsop and Mrs Tucker had started to cry.

In a deep, gravelly voice, the old witch boomed, "I am MRS ABERCROMBIE, rightful queen of Witch Island! Miserable humans, you are POWERLESS before me! If you want to see your children again, you'd better bring me Old Noshie and Skirty Marm!"

In an explosion of black smoke that left everybody coughing, she vanished. Iron shutters clanged across the doors and windows of the cottage. The panic-stricken parents rushed forward, banging on doors and thumping on windows. They screamed the children's names, they begged Mrs Abercrombie to take pity on them.

It was useless. Though they hated to leave their children, there was only one thing to do.

They rushed through the shadowy forest to the vicarage.

"Good gracious!" choked Mr Snelling when he heard the awful news. "The witches were right all along! Besides our children, that ghastly Mrs Abercrombie has got my Mendax! Oh, what on earth are we going to do?"

"We tried to warn you about that Mrs Brightpie," Old Noshie could not help saying. "Well, it's too late now."

Mrs Blenkinsop began to cry again.

"Shut up, Nosh," said Skirty Marm. "You're making them depressed."

The frantic parents of Tranters End were jammed into the vicarage sitting-room. Old Noshie and Skirty Marm felt dreadfully sorry for them. They were sitting on top of the piano because the room was so full. PC Bloater sat on the piano-stool taking notes – but nobody really thought there was anything the police could do.

"Look, I don't understand this stuff about a Hat," growled Mr Noggs. "And I don't care! If that's what Mrs Abercrombie wants – let her have it! All I want is my Amy!"

There were murmurs of agreement from the other parents. Old Noshie and Skirty Marm were very worried. These humans were in no mood to hear excuses about Witch Island politics. What did they care about witches' democracy when their children had been stolen?

Mr Snelling held up his hand for quiet. "If we give Mrs Abercrombie the Power Hat," he said tearfully, "we'll be putting Mendax and the witches in *terrible danger*."

"Our children are in terrible danger already!" cried Mrs Blenkinsop. "There isn't any choice!"

"But we can't trust the word of that dreadful witch," argued Mr Babbercorn. "What if she gets the Hat – and keeps the children?"

"Skirty Marm," Alice said, "can't the Power Hat help us?"

Skirty Marm shook her head. The bobble on the disguised Power Hat wobbled forlornly.

"It's all a question of knowing how to use the Hat," she explained. "I have to give it a proper COMMAND – and that would take a gigantic lot of magic."

"Maybe you're depending too much on the Hat," Mr Babbercorn said. "You're intelligent witches – there must be something you can do without it!"

Old Noshie sighed. "Two witches can't do anything against Mrs A. – not when they don't know how to work the Hat!"

"Yes," said Mr Babbercorn excitedly, "but what about more than two witches? What about FIFTY?"

"Eh?" gasped Old Noshie and Skirty Marm.

"Ask your FRIENDS for help!" Mr Babbercorn cried. "They surely don't want Mrs Abercrombie to be their queen again?"

Skirty Marm leapt off the piano as if someone had given her an electric shock.

"You're right! Our old pals from the Island will help us!"

"We must hurry," said Old Noshie, scrambling down clumsily. "Today's Hallowe'en, don't forget! They'll be taking off on their broomsticks soon, to go and bother the humans!"

"But we can't spare any time!" cried Mrs Tucker.

Alice patted her shoulder kindly. "Please give the witches a chance. If we'd listened to them in the first place, this would never have happened."

Old Noshie and Skirty Marm were already hurrying through the dark garden towards the shed. Mendax had hidden a secret radio to Witch Island here during his spying days. He had stopped being a spy ages ago, but he still used the radio to keep in contact with his cat-friends at home.

Skirty Marm lit the end of her finger for light (witches can do this easily, without hurting themselves) and held the little cat-sized headphones against one ear.

"Come in, Witch Island! Skirty Marm calling Witch Island! Mayday! Mayday!"

Over the radio came a crackling voice.

"Witch Island here. Come in, Skirty Marm."

It took Skirty several minutes of long-distance

argument before she was put in touch with Chancellor Badsleeves. The Chancellor had been democratically elected after the downfall of the queen and she was now the most important witch on the island. Luckily, she had once had the next-door cave to Old Noshie and Skirty Marm, and she was not a witch to forget old friends.

"Hello, you two!" Badsleeves called cheerfully over the radio. "Happy Hallowe'en!"

As quickly as she could, Skirty Marm told Badsleeves about the terrible situation in Tranters End.

"We need your help to save the children!"

There was a pause.

"Of course, I'd *like* to help," said Badsleeves slowly. "But it's Hallowe'en! We're supposed to be out *annoying* the humans, not *rescuing* them! The other witches aren't going to like this one bit – I'll never get it past them!"

"You dratted politicians, you're all the same!" shouted Skirty Marm. "All you care about is VOTES! Well, you listen to me, Badsleeves – if you don't help, we'll have to give Mrs A. the Power Hat! And once she gets her hands on it, you'll lose a lot more than votes!"

"For instance, HEADS," put in Old Noshie.

"The question is," Skirty Marm said sternly, "do you want Mrs A. to be your queen again?"

There was a long, thoughtful silence.

"Leave it to me," said Badsleeves.

One hour later – to the amazement of the villagers – there was a hand-picked flying broom squadron camped on the vicarage lawn. Chancellor Badsleeves and fifty of her finest witches sat in groups around five camp fires. The flickering flames made their tattered black figures look very sinister. Though the people of Tranters End knew they had come to help, they could not help being nervous. Alice shivered and held baby Thomas very tight. Could these witches rescue the children?

Mr Babbercorn bravely shook hands with Chancellor Badsleeves – he recognized her from a photograph Noshie and Skirty had loyally hung in their belfry. She was a stout, stumpy witch with short white hair and round glasses.

"This is very kind of you," he said.

"Well, it was hard to give up our Hallowe'en," said Badsleeves. "But this is our battle too. Don't worry, we'll get your little humans back."

"Do it NOW!" called Mr Noggs. "I want my Amy!"

"Patience, human!" Badsleeves said, not unkindly. "We need to plan our attack. And this is an army that flies on its stomach. We need something to eat!"

At last, the anxious people of Tranters End had something definite to do. They hurried back to their houses to gather food for fifty-one hungry witches. It was an odd mixture. PC Bloater brought some dead mice from the mouse-trap at the police station. Mrs Tucker brought a large trifle. Mrs Blenkinsop brought two packets of Weetabix, and Alice filled an old tin bath with gallons of butterscotch Instant Whip.

Badsleeves and her flying squad had never eaten human food before, but they gobbled up everything they were offered. They particularly liked the Instant Whip and the conkers brought by Mr Noggs.

Mr Babbercorn and Mr Snelling went from campfire to campfire, carrying buckets of heated water from the muddy village pond.

"Cor, that hits the spot!" said Badsleeves, licking her lips. "You've certainly taught them how to make a proper cup of witch tea!"

Old Noshie stared at a huddled, dusty figure, sitting apart from the others. "What's Mouldypage doing here?"

Mouldypage was the ancient keeper of the Witch Island State Library. She was a brilliant scholar and the only witch as old and clever as Mrs Abercrombie – they had been at school together. Mouldypage had helped the humans once before, but she was an eccentric witch and you could never predict what side she would be on.

"Has she come to help?" Skirty Marm asked hopefully.

"I don't know," admitted Badsleeves. "She just insisted on coming along. Every time I ask her what she's up to, she tells me to mind my own business."

The three witches watched, as PC Bloater approached Mouldypage with a tray of refreshments.

"Would you like a mouse – er – Madam?"

"Ah," croaked Mouldypage, "you must be the local centurion."

"What's she talking about?" asked Old Noshie.

"She hasn't visited this land since the Romans were in charge," explained Badsleeves. "She doesn't realize times have changed."

She popped a chocolate biscuit into her mouth, burped loudly and shouted, "Gather round, flying squad! Gather round, humans! Here's the PLAN!"

8

Ambush

Mrs Abercrombie opened the cellar door. Huffing and puffing, she stomped down hundreds and hundreds of stone steps. Beneath the cottage she had dug out a huge underground cave. It was chilly and damp and lit only by eerie, greenish, magical lights.

The children of Tranters End were sitting in a frightened huddle against the slimy wall. They had been thrown into the cave as soon as they arrived for the party. Little Amy Noggs was crying, and Emma Blenkinsop had her arm around her.

"Stop that noise," said Mrs Abercrombie. "I've come to tell you what's happening. If Old Noshie and Skirty Marm give me my Power Hat, you're all free. And if they don't – well, I eat you all. Us OLDER witches still enjoy eating a nice, plump human child."

"This is the worst Hallowe'en party I've ever been to," said Ben Blenkinsop.

"Well, it'll teach you not to go near gingerbread houses," said Mrs Abercrombie, "you greedy little pigs!"

"You'll be arrested for this!" shouted Ben bravely.

"There's nothing to worry about," said Mrs Abercrombie. "As long as your parents love you enough to get my Hat."

"Of course they love us enough!" yelled Danny, the oldest Blenkinsop child. "And they HATE you! You'll be sorry when my mum gets hold of you!"

Mrs Abercrombie looked down at the alarm clock that was tied to her wrist with string. "Ah, that cloaking spell has nearly worn off. Suppertime!"

Laughing horribly, she vanished in a cloud of smelly purple smoke.

She had very much enjoyed frightening the children (though she wished more of them had been crying) and was in a jaunty mood when she appeared, in another puff of smoke, in her kitchen.

"Five minutes, cat!" she chortled, twanging

the bars of Mendax's cage. "And then you'll be in my cauldron!"

Poor Mendax had resigned himself to being eaten. He sighed. "I don't suppose I could make a suggestion about how to serve me? I'm too skinny to roast nicely, but if I'm done slowly in a casserole—"

"SILENCE!" thundered Mrs Abercrombie. "How dare you take that insolent tone with your QUEEN?"

"I'd like to point out," said Mendax, "that at the moment, you're not my queen – or anybody else's."

"I'm as good as crowned already!" snapped Mrs Abercrombie. "I've finally won back my Power Hat!"

Suddenly, a loud voice outside cried, "We've got you SURROUNDED! Come out with your hands up!"

It was Badsleeves, shouting through a megaphone she had borrowed from PC Bloater.

"NEVER!" screamed Mrs Abercrombie. "You can't do anything to ME!"

She looked wildly round the kitchen and kicked Mrs Wilkins, who was snoring beside the fire.

"Wake up! We're surrounded – and you've got to fight!"

"I'm not being paid for no fighting," grumbled Mrs Wilkins.

"You'll go straight back to prison if they catch you!" shouted Mrs Abercrombie.

"Best place for her, in my opinion," said Mendax.

Mrs Abercrombie gave his cage a brutal shove, which knocked him off his four paws. "I'll deal with you later, cat-slave!"

It was all over in a moment.

There were witches on super-powered broomsticks in every tree around the cottage. Two witches waited on the roof, ready to leap down the chimney. The humans were on the ground, armed with saucepans and rolling-pins.

At a signal from Badsleeves, a hundred bolts of heavy magic smashed against the iron shutters and reduced them to dust. With blood-curdling shrieks, the flying witches swooped.

Mrs Abercrombie was a clever old witch and horribly strong, but without the special protection of the Power Hat she was no match for the fifty hand-picked witches of the flying squad. Twenty of them held her down, while the humans tied her arms and legs with a thick rope. She wriggled furiously, like a gigantic, angry slug.

Mrs Wilkins was caught trying to sneak away up the chimney. She was arrested and tied up next to Mrs Abercrombie.

"You said there wouldn't be any danger!" she shouted. "That's the last time I vote for YOU!"

"Where are the children?" clamoured the villagers. "Give us our children – you FIEND!"

Mendax jumped on his hind legs and grabbed the bars of his cage with his front paws.

"Noshie! Skirty! In the cellar!"

Old Noshie and Skirty Marm were having the time of their lives. Skirty had always dreamed of flying with the Number One Broom Squadron, known on Witch Island as the "Death-or-Glory Brooms". With whoops of triumph, they wrenched open the cellar door and hurtled down the hundreds of steps to the secret cave.

Poor Amy Noggs screamed to see more witchy figures looming through the shadows. But Emma Blenkinsop recognized her two friends from the Brownies at once.

"We're safe!" she cried, giving each witch a hug. "We knew you'd come for us!"

"Mrs A. can't beat US!" boasted Skirty Marm. "Not while I'm wearing the Power Hat!"

"What's so special about that old thing?" asked Ben Blenkinsop. "It looks like a tea cosy."

"You'll find out," chuckled Old Noshie. "Come on, let's get you out of here."

The two witches led the children up the stone steps to the cottage kitchen. There were cries of joy as they ran into the arms of their parents.

"Thank you! Thank you!" Mr Babbercorn shook Badsleeves's hand so hard that her hat fell off. "You're our heroines!"

"I don't normally hold with magic," said Mr Noggs, "but you've been very helpful."

"Hear hear!" said all the other humans.

"YEUCH!" complained Mrs Abercrombie. "Disgusting human MUSH – no self-respecting witch would have stood it in my day!"

But Badsleeves and her flying squad looked rather pleased. Nobody had ever thanked them before or called them heroines. It was certainly a very unusual way to spend Hallowe'en.

"What shall we do with Mrs A.?" asked Old Noshie.

"We could kill her," suggested Badsleeves. "It

seems a pity not to have that State Funeral – I've already written my speech."

"You won't kill me!" raged Mrs Abercrombie. "Because I've got one more thing you want!"

She pursed up her rubbery lips until they looked like the nozzle of a vacuum-cleaner. Then she sucked hard. The door of Mendax's cage flew open. The little cat clung on with all his might, but it was useless. He was sucked right across the room and Mrs Abercrombie, with a loud gulp, swallowed him whole.

"You nasty, evil, beastly, wicked—" gasped the vicar, turning deathly pale.

"You could always have him back," said Mrs Abercrombie, "if you swap him for the HAT!"

"No way!" said Badsleeves firmly.

"Please!" begged poor Mr Snelling. "Mendax ran away to protect the witches because he knew he was powerless once Mrs Abercrombie got his code! Please don't desert him now!"

The witches tried everything.

Watched by the sniffing vicar, the fifty witches and the terrified villagers, they tried finding spells, rescue spells, shrinking spells (for Mendax) and stun spells (for Mrs Abercrombie). Old Noshie even tried jumping up and down on Mrs Abercrombie's stomach. Nothing worked.

Sorry, typed the Power Hat. *He's inside her, and even my magic cannot touch him.*

"Oh, Mendax!" cried the vicar. "Are you in pain? Can you hear me?"

"Let's be thankful for small mercies," said the muffled voice of Mendax from inside the ex-queen's stomach. "At least she didn't chew me."

"Give me my Hat," said Mrs Abercrombie, "and I'll let him go."

"Don't you dare!" shouted Badsleeves. "Human children are one matter, but I'm not losing my government for the sake of a CAT!"

"The Chancellor is right," Mendax's voice said bravely. "What is one small cat against the freedom of Witch Island? You'd better leave me here, to be DIGESTED."

"We appreciate this, Cat," said Badsleeves. "I shall order a statue to be built for you."

"Something simple in black marble, perhaps," said Mendax. "Yes, that would be very nice. It's a slow, horrible death, but I am happy to lay down my poor life for the sake of the Greater Good."

"You always were a noble cat," said poor Mr Snelling. "I'm going to miss you so much, I think my heart will break!"

"Think of me sometimes," said Mendax. "Put a little stone in some shady nook. And on it write these simple words –

Stranger! Pause and shed a Tear for
MENDAX
("Colonel Mendy" of Fungus Gulch)
Revoltingly DIGESTED
For the Cause of LIBERTY!"

"Oh, that's beautiful!" said Mr Snelling, busily writing it down in his notebook.

All the villagers, and even several of the hand-picked witches, sniffed.

"Typical Mendax!" murmured Mr Babbercorn to Alice, wiping his eyes. "I'd swear he's enjoying this!"

Mrs Abercrombie laughed nastily. "You won't be able to stand his screams of agony for long! You'll soon be BEGGING me to take the Hat!"

"Fiddlesticks!" grunted an ancient dusty voice. "You always were a power-mad witch, Euphemia Abercrombie – and it's time you were taught a lesson."

The dusty cobwebby figure of Mouldypage shuffled through the crowd.

For the very first time, Mrs Abercrombie looked alarmed. She had been at school with Mouldypage, and no living witch knew her better.

"You think you're so clever," said Mouldypage. "You think you know everything about the Power Hat."

"I know more than you do!" blustered Mrs Abercrombie. "I won the Golden Broom at school!"

"Only because you CHEATED," said Mouldypage with a dry chuckle. "Some things never change! I didn't much care at the time, because I was only interested in books. But Witch Island is much more comfortable now you've gone. So I think I should remind you who's REALLY the smartest witch of all!"

She turned to Skirty Marm.

"Ignorant Red-Stocking," she croaked. "This is an emergency. You must ask the Power Hat for a page of the FORBIDDEN BOOK."

"NO!" bellowed Mrs Abercrombie. She began to thrash about madly in her ropes. "You're bluffing – the Forbidden Book doesn't exist!"

Trembling with excitement, Skirty Marm shut her eyes. The green letters were already inside her head.

Yes! At last – someone who knows how to use me properly! the Power Hat had typed. *Now, pay attention . . .*

A breathless silence fell over the cottage. Witches and humans watched as Skirty Marm read the Hat's instructions.

When Skirty Marm opened her eyes, she was very pale.

"Untie Mrs Abercrombie!"

All the witches began to babble and shriek with fury.

"You're CRAZY!" shouted Badsleeves. "She'll kill us all!"

"Noshie," said Skirty Marm, "untie her!"

Old Noshie did not like it any more than the others – but she trusted Skirty Marm. Shaking like a pale green jelly, she undid the ex-queen's ropes.

"Mrs Abercrombie," said Skirty Marm solemnly, "hand over Mendax – and you can have the Hat!"

"Leave me here!" Mendax cried, from inside the Royal stomach. "I'm only a little lying cat! What am I worth when weighed against the lives of all these witches?"

A deathly hush suddenly fell over all the witches.

"I've shut them up with a temporary silence spell," said Mouldypage. "I can't stand noise. Now, get on with it, Red-Stocking!"

Mrs Abercrombie was breathing hard, as if she had been running. "Come to me, beloved Power Hat!" she panted. "Together, we will reign in WICKEDNESS!"

Skirty Marm slowly took the Power Hat off her head and held it out to Mrs Abercrombie.

Five of the silenced witches fainted.

Her face alight with terrible joy, Mrs Abercrombie gave a mighty burp and Mendax shot out of her mouth. With a "miaow" of shock, he landed in the arms of the vicar.

Mrs Abercrombie's hairy fist closed around the Power Hat. And then an extraordinary thing happened.

The bobble of the Hat burst into a ball of scarlet flame. The flames consumed the rest of the Hat, and Mrs Abercrombie dropped it with a yelp of pain. The blazing Power Hat slowly rose into the air. For a moment, it burned so brightly that everyone had to shade their eyes. Then it crumbled away into black cinders – and disappeared.

On the empty air, a thread of black smoke briefly formed the word

"GOODBYE".

The amazed silence stretched on and on, even when Mouldypage removed her spell.

"Gone!" whispered Chancellor Badsleeves in amazement. "The greatest treasure of our Island

– and our greatest CURSE! Gone!"

"The Power Hat didn't mean to be a curse," Skirty Marm said loyally. "It only did bad things because Mrs A. made it!"

"And since it lived with these humans," added Old Noshie, "it wanted to be good."

"How disgusting!" muttered Mouldypage. "Dratted humans and their SOPPY ways!"

"You don't approve of us, yet you've been very kind to us!" Mr Snelling said. He was stroking Mendax and smiling all over his round face. "We're so grateful!"

"Oh, I didn't do it for you," croaked Mouldypage. "I wanted to get my own back on Euphemia Abercrombie. I would have won that Golden Broom if she hadn't nicked my best spell. Well, we're even now, Euphemia – that'll teach you to snoop in other people's pencil cases!"

Mrs Abercrombie had not made one sound since the vanishing of the Power Hat. Her hideous face had turned an unhealthy yellow.

"Gone!" she choked. "My life's work – ruined! Old Noshie and Skirty Marm, you'll PAY for this!"

"Take no notice," said Mouldypage. "She'll need all her magic when I've finished with her!"

She gabbled a spell in witch-Latin. There was just enough time to see Mrs Abercrombie's expression of terror before the two ancient witches vanished into thin air.

Witches and humans were left in the cottage kitchen, staring at the space where the evil ex-queen had been.

Mr Babbercorn was the first to recover. He hugged Old Noshie and Skirty Marm.

"Please forgive me for not listening to your warning," he said. "There's a lot I still don't understand about all this – for instance, how did you know Mrs Brightpie had Mendax? How did he get the message to you?"

"We might as well tell the truth now," said Old Noshie.

"You're rubbish at keeping secrets!" grumbled Skirty Marm.

"I'm afraid we cast a small spell on Thomas," Noshie said.

"A spell!" gasped Alice.

"Well, it was actually quite a big spell. To make him understand animals. That's how he got the message."

"It's his christening present," confessed Skirty Marm. "We just couldn't bear to give him something ordinary. Please don't be cross!"

Alice hugged Thomas – she was carrying him in a sling around her neck. To the surprise of the two guilty witches, she and Mr Babbercorn started laughing.

"I should be cross," said Alice. "But I don't mind him keeping this present as long as you promise not to cast any more spells on him!"

"Hurrah!" cried Thomas – a piece of Babyspeak that everyone understood.

"We promise!" chorused the witches.

Mr Noggs had been whispering with the other humans. He stepped forward, clearing his throat importantly.

"Ladies and – er – witches," he said. "We realize that you have missed your usual Hallowe'en Ball, through helping us. As a mark of our gratitude, we'd like to give you a *party*."

And this is how the most unusual Hallowe'en party in the world was held, in the vicarage garden of Tranters End.

Mr Snelling telephoned the jazz band that sometimes played in the local pub. Alice made another tub of Instant Whip. Everyone in the village cleared larders and fridges to give Badsleeves and her witches the greatest feast of their lives. Old Noshie and Skirty Marm threw themselves into mad witch-dances round the blazing bonfires. They taught Mr Babbercorn the Donkey-Dive, the Ear-Grabber and other traditional dances. He enjoyed it very much and only stopped when someone shouted, "Take your partners for the SLOW BUM-KICK!"

"This is the best Hallowe'en Ball since you two sang your song!" declared Chancellor Badsleeves. "I'm going to have trouble scaring this lot next year!"

Old Noshie and Skirty Marm grinned.

"Oh, humans are all right," said Skirty Marm.

"When you get to know them," added Old Noshie.

Kate Saunders
BELFRY WITCHES 2
Mendax the Mystery Cat

Old Noshie and Skirty Marm have been trying terribly hard to be good. They've only done the tiniest bit of magic, they haven't touched a drop of Nasty Medicine, and they've even been learning how to knit!

But strange powers are at work in Tranters End. First there's the underwear that comes to life, then the flying pigs – and then a very mysterious black cat arrives at the vicarage door . . .

Kate Saunders
BELFRY WITCHES 3
Red Stocking Rescue

Old Noshie and Skirty Marm are terribly upset. Although they've promised to be good, Mr Babbercorn won't let them be bridesmaids at his wedding. And Mendax the cat isn't even allowed to sing a solo!

But then deep, dark magic turns Alice, Mr Babbercorn's bride-to-be, into a snail. Who is the culprit – and can two brave witches (and one clever cat) cook up a spell that will save the wedding from disaster?

Kate Saunders
BELFRY WITCHES 5
Witch You Were Here

Old Noshie and Skirty Marm are outraged. Mr Babbercorn plans to take his wife and baby son on holiday – and he doesn't want any magical friends in tow!

Aided by a time machine and their trusty broomsticks, the witches plan a bigger, better holiday of their own – a mad mystery tour to the Upright Tower of Pisa and the Mona Noshie, the world's most famous painting. But the happy holidaymakers are being followed . . .

Kate Saunders
BELFRY WITCHES 6
Broomsticks in Space

A strange light has been seen in the night sky over Tranters End. Could it be a new planet? Maybe that would explain the weird weather – surely snow in summer isn't normal!

Something very dirty and dangerous is afoot, and Old Noshie and Skirty Marm are certain who's to blame – none other than their old enemy Mrs Abercrombie. For the deadliest witch of all has moved her operations to outer space, and this time she's cooking up a king-sized cauldron of trouble!

Collect all the BELFRY WITCHES books!

The prices shown below are correct at the time of going to press. However, Macmillan Publishers reserve the right to show new retail prices on covers which may differ from those previously advertised.

KATE SAUNDERS

1. A Spell of Witches	0 330 37282 3	£2.99
2. Mendax the Mystery Cat	0 330 37283 1	£2.99
3. Red Stocking Rescue	0 330 37284 X	£2.99
4. Power Hat Panic	0 330 37285 8	£2.99
5. Witch You Were Here	0 330 37286 6	£2.99
6. Broomsticks in Space	0 330 37287 4	£2.99

All Macmillan titles can be ordered at your local bookshop or are available by post from:

Book Service by Post
PO Box 29, Douglas, Isle of Man IM99 1BQ

Credit cards accepted. For details:
Telephone: 01624 675137
Fax: 01624 670923
E-mail: bookshop@enterprise.net

Free postage and packing in the UK.
Overseas customers: add £1 per book (paperback)
and £3 per book (hardback).